MYSTERY AT POINT BEACH

~ Book 4 ~

Bushwhacked

Kate Jungwirth

Deborah Erdmann

Though the lingering rays of the sunset

Are forgotten by morn's early birth

And the leaves in the dead of the winter

Yaw and sprawl as they plummet to earth

Even so, think of me in the stillness

In the memories of mirth and of shame

Think of me, though my shadow has withered

Forget me not and remember my name

Ray Anderson

CHAPTER 1

A veil of mist clung to the towering pine trees, blurring my vision as I raced through the dense forest. Twigs snapped beneath the massive paws chasing after me, a loud roar piercing the air.

The hunter was closing in on its prey. His hot breath prickled the back of my neck, sending fear and adrenaline coursing through my veins.

Suddenly, I lost my footing, caught up in a land-slide that sent me rolling downhill. I landed abruptly at the bottom of a ravine in a field of tiny blue flowers.

An old metal trunk stood in the clearing; a rusted arrow engraved along the top. Just as I lifted the lid, the bear came crashing through the trees. I quickly climbed inside, but the trunk was bottomless, and I found myself falling through time and space before finally hitting the ground with a thud.

Opening my eyes, I realized it was all a dream. I

was lying on the floor of my grandpa's camper, still wrapped in my blanket.

"Grandpa, wake up!"

"What's wrong, Dominic?" He sat up so fast that his head nearly hit the roof.

"I just had the worst nightmare ever." I got off the floor and crawled back into bed.

"Take a deep breath, everything's fine." He rushed to my side. "Do you want to tell me about it?"

I shrunk under my covers. "I dreamt a bear was chasing me through the woods," I said, glancing around the room. "What time is it?"

"It's just after midnight."

The blackened trees bending in the wind outside my window at the foot of my bed looked like monsters. "Where are we, GB"? (GB is short for Grandpa Bob.)

"We're camping at Point Beach in Two Rivers, remember?" He rubbed the sleep from his eyes. "I bet one of your mom's cookies will make you feel better."

He rustled around in the small kitchenette, returning with a plate of cookies.

"Thanks, Grandpa." I took a big bite. "Got milk?"

"There's the 13-year-old boy I remember. Thank heaven you still have your imagination."

He padded back to the mini fridge for the milk, poured some into a paper cup and handed it to me. "Nothing like milk to calm a person."

I downed the milk, then settled back into my pillow.

"Get some sleep, Dominic. Things always look better in the morning."

Somehow, I doubted that. Deep down inside, the dream was clanging around in my head. Something dark and dangerous was lurking at Point Beach.

Sunlight filtered through the screen windows of our rustic Nimrod camper, rousing me from my sleep. I stretched, glancing around the canvas, mildew-stained walls to try and see where GB was.

As I made my way to his cot, I was alarmed to

find him still lying in it. He didn't normally sleep this late. And I should mention … he didn't appear to be alive. I frantically shook him. "Grandpa!"

He rolled toward me, slowly opening one baby blue.

"Dominic! Did you have another dream?"

I breathed a sigh of relief. "Sorry about that, GB. You scared me. I thought you were dead."

"Good grief, boy. I may be old, but I'm not dead, at least not yet." GB scrubbed his hand over his face. "What time is it?"

I glanced at the rectangular, battery-operated clock that rested on the counter. "It's 8:15. Geez, GB. You're sleeping the day away." I couldn't resist teasing him with the same line he always uses on me. "Is it okay if I ride my bike on the trails?"

GB set one foot on the floor. "Slow down, Dominic. Let me cook up some grub to start your day right."

I already had my Nikes on. "I'm still full from last night's cookies. Can I eat when I get back?"

"I guess that's okay, but don't be gone too long.

Windsong and the kids should be here soon."

I was excited to see my friends from Chicago again. GB and I had started a yearly tradition of camping with Windsong and her grandkids at Point Beach. Forest, Sailor and I even solved a few mysteries here the past few years.

My lime green Trek was parked where I left it last night, by the pumphouse. A shiver ran through me as I recalled last fall when Ranger Rick was kidnapped and left bound and gagged inside the old, stone structure.

Ranger Rick is my nemesis. It seems every time we're trying to solve a crime, he interferes.

The good news is that now there's a new assistant ranger. Her name is Sally, and she seems to have a *thing* for Ranger Rick. I can't tell if he enjoys her constant hovering, or if he just likes having another person there to boss around.

Cruising along, I had just passed the outdoor chapel on the left, when a huge bumble bee approached. I tried pedaling faster, but he kept up the pace. He was near my head, now. Good thing I was wearing a baseball cap. It offered at least a little protection.

I swatted at it, losing my grip on the handlebars, along with my balance. Unable to stop, I found myself careening off the trail and sailing through the woods. My Trek shifted to the right and crashed into a tree, launching me headfirst into a clump of bushes.

Stunned and sore all over, I slowly stood to my feet. I had never seen this part of the park before. The forest was dense, which cast a dark shadow on the landscape. There was wild ivy growing on the trees, and thick foliage. It looked like a jungle.

Making my way back to my bike, I noticed a rusty axe wedged in a tree. *That seems odd.*

Approaching it, I stubbed my toe on what felt like a rock. As I bent down to take a closer look, I saw a sheet of solid metal that was partially hidden by overgrown weeds. Pushing the weeds aside, it seemed the metal structure was bigger than I first thought.

What on earth was *this* doing here? I brushed

away the dirt, ivy, and mossy growth covering the top.

Eureka! On the right side was a brass ring over what must be the hatch. Grabbing ahold of the rusty handle I pulled with all my might. Nothing happened. I tried using both my hands, willing the door to open. Finally, the hatch pulled up, so quickly I fell backward.

I inched toward the circular hole and peered down into total blackness. *This must be some kind of bunker. Better come back with a flashlight.* I put the cover back down, and then carefully concealed the roof with the leaves and moss I had initially removed. Something told me this needed to be kept secret.

I wiped my dirty hands onto my jeans. *That's gonna leave a stain.* Good thing GB and I were roughing it.

As I left the area, my sixth sense went on alert. I looked over my shoulder a few times, thinking I heard twigs cracking behind the bushes, but didn't see anything. I started to feel spooked.

CHAPTER 2

I raced back to my campsite. I was excited about my discovery, but it was my craving for GB's homestyle cooking that caused me to ride like the wind.

"GB!" I yelled, as I hopped off my bike and headed for Nimrod. My nose told me he was inside, by the smell of bacon frying.

"Land sakes, Dominic. How did you manage to get so dirty in such a short amount of time?" He took one look at my pants and shook his head.

"Sorry. Is it okay if I change my clothes after breakfast? I'm starving!"

"Sure. Take a seat," he said, loading my plate with some sort of slimy goop.

"Gross! What the heck is this, Grandpa?" I wrinkled my nose.

GB grinned. "These are grits. They're made from corn. You need to try some!"

"No thanks. I like my corn on the cob, where it belongs. Can I just have bacon?"

"Okay, but you can't make a meal on bacon. Let's get you some cereal, too." He reached for the box from the cabinet above the sink while I grabbed the milk from the fridge.

I took a seat at the table and began wolfing down the Wheaties while GB drank his coffee.

"After breakfast I want to see if Forest and Sailor are here. Did Windsong happen to tell you what site they're on?"

"No. I called her yesterday, but she wasn't able to talk because she was taking a bath."

"That's weird."

"Why is it weird?"

"If someone called me, I wouldn't tell them I'm taking a bath. It's embarrassing."

"With the number of baths you take, the chances of that happening are slim."

Haha. Very funny.

Since I didn't know which site they were on, I had no choice but to bike through the campground and see if I could spot Windsong's retro trailer. She's a bona fide gypsy. She wears Bohemian skirts, peasant tops and flowers in her hair.

While passing by the camp host site, I decided to stop in. I figured Mr. and Mrs. Buckley might have some idea where Windsong was.

The Buckleys are Floridians at heart, at least by the looks of their gaudy campsite décor; green-wired palm trees and pink flamingos were scattered about. As I approached their site, I noticed they had added a neon-colored sign that read "Margaritaville." *Nice.*

Sadie Buckley sat at the picnic table, shelling peas. Her poodle, Sprinkles, was crunching on the pea pods she had tossed on the ground. It looked like her husband, Bert, had dozed off by the way he was slouched in their golf cart.

"Hi, Mrs. Buckley!" I parked my bike and joined her at the table.

"Darren! So nice to see you back at Point Beach. How have you been?" She ruffled her greyish-blue bouffant updo.

Mrs. B. never gets my name right. I just play along.

"I'm good. I'm actually looking for Windsong and my friends. Do you know which site they're on?" I reached down to pat Sprinkles on the head.

"I'm afraid I don't know. Bert might have an idea, but he's taking a nap. Going into town for tuna and cheddar cheese for my salad really wore him out. Not to mention picking up these peas—fresh from the farmer's market."

"Cool. So, what's new at the campground this summer? Anything mysterious I should know about?"

The Buckleys had played a part in helping solve some mysteries here the past few years. They like to stay on top of things.

"Actually, there is some news." She tossed a handful of peas into the dish and pushed it aside. "A bear was spotted this morning, south of Point Beach, in the woods!" Her eyes widened behind her thick glasses. "Ranger Rick is holding a meeting at the nature center tomorrow at 9:00. You should all try and attend."

"Wow! That *is* big news. I'll be sure to tell the others all about the bear on the loose."

I got back on my bike. "Say hi to Mr. Buckley for me when he wakes up."

As I pedaled down the road, the thought came to me that my dream might have something to do with the bear. I suddenly had a sick feeling in my stomach.

I spotted Windsong's lime green trailer on site 108, just down the road. She was putting up her neon-flowered lights. Forest and Sailor came running out of the trailer when they saw me.

They didn't get a chance to say hello before I blurted out the news. "You guys, guess what? There's a bear in the park, and tomorrow the ranger is holding a meeting at the nature center!"

"Oh, my goodness! Well, don't get too worked up, Dominic. Bears usually avoid people, and if we don't bother them, they won't bother us." Windsong must've seen the ghostly pale color my face had turned. "Come here for a hug."

Hugging isn't my thing, but you can't say no to Windsong. She grabbed me for a quick bear hug, giving me a kiss on the head before I could pull away. Her white braids smelled like incense. The kind they use at funerals.

Sailor came in for a hug too, but I held up my hand to high-five her—my way of avoiding another hug. Same old Sailor. Long, unruly hair, flip-flops and mismatched clothes.

"Windsong, is it okay if Forest joins me on a bike ride?" I was anxious to show him the bunker.

"That's fine, let me whip up a snack for you to take along." She started walking toward her trailer.

"That's okay, I have Lunchables in my backpack."

Lunchables? Ugh. I'm so bad at lying, but I would rather starve than eat whatever concoction Windsong came up with. I wonder how Forest and Sailor survived her cooking.

She nodded. "Be back in time for dinner, then. I'm making Thai pineapple rice."

Forest grabbed his red Yeti Mountain bike and hopped on. We started to take off when Sailor whined behind us.

"Ooh, wait for me!"

I was about to ixnay that idea but thought better of it. Sometimes Sailor actually has something intelligent to say. Though, if she wore sensible shoes, I might think more highly of her.

"Fine, Sailor. Get your bike."

"Have you already found a mystery to solve?" Forest asked while we waited.

"As a matter of fact, I have. You're not going to believe what I found buried underground!"

"Try me."

"Sure, but first can you grab a flashlight?"

After Sailor pulled up on her bike and Forest returned with a flashlight, we headed to Ridges Trail, following in the same direction I went that morning. It seemed like we were biking forever. I was short of breath, Forest was swatting at mosquitos, and Sailor was humming a Kelly Clarkson tune behind us.

Had I lost my bearings? After what felt like an eternity, I was relieved to recognize the jungle-like mess of leaves and ivy to the right.

"This way!" I started pedaling into the woods, but then remembered my crash earlier and got off my bike. We'd have to proceed on foot.

Finally, I saw the axe in the tree.

"Here it is!" I cleared away the leaves and debris.

"Whoa!" Forest knelt down on the metal top of the bunker.

"This is amazing!" Sailor stared in wonder at the beast of a box.

"Okay, so how do we get in?"

I yanked on the handle and lifted the hatch. We all peered down into the dark hole.

CHAPTER 3

"What do you think is in there?" Sailor bent down to the point where she almost fell in head-first.

"Look out!" Forest pulled her back.

"I'll go first, and then you guys can follow." I grabbed the flashlight from my backpack and lowered myself into the dark tunnel. The steps were barely wide enough to fit my Nikes, much less get a good grip on. I stuck the flashlight in my mouth, using my teeth to hold it, and continued the downward climb.

A daddy longlegs crept toward me. Spiders I can handle, but what I can't handle is rats. I can deal with snakes, toads and those annoying yippy dogs. Anything but rats. When my right foot hit the ground, I breathed a sigh of relief.

"I'm in!"

Forest peered down at me. "What's it like?"

"It's black as midnight, and it reeks in here!" The

musty odor was overpowering. I wondered how long the bunker had been unoccupied.

"Shine the light up here so we can come down." Forest began making his descent, followed by Sailor, although she seemed a little reluctant at first.

"Help! A tarantula is trying to jump on me!" Sailor practically slid down the steps, landing with a thud at the bottom.

"It's only a daddy longlegs," I said.

That's Sailor alright, God love 'er.

I pointed my flashlight into the dark compartment. A shabby brown rug was strewn across the cement floor. On the left, a makeshift bookcase filled the entire wall, and on the right was a cot, covered with a dark green patchwork quilt; a red-and-black checkered flannel shirt lying across it. The pillow was yellowed and stained.

A rusted kerosene lamp sat on a small, wooden table in the middle of the room, next to a deck of old Green Bay Packer playing cards in the center and an unfinished game of solitaire spread out on top.

"Dude! What kind of caveman lived in here?" Forest walked over to the bookshelf, gingerly picking up a *Field and Stream* magazine that was covered in spider webs. "Wow, this magazine is from 1937!"

I made my way over to him. Next to a book with the title *Where the mounting of Hunting Trophies Attains Perfection*, was a tan, weathered old book. I blew the dust off it, which made me sneeze. The yellowed pages were filled with handwritten notes. "Hey, it's a journal!"

Forest and Sailor leaned in closer.

I opened it and shined the flashlight on the inscription inside the cover— *"This journal belongs to Lumberjack Ray Anderson."*

"A lumberjack's diary? How romantic!" Sailor's eyelashes fluttered.

"Maybe the dead lumberjack can be your boyfriend." Forest threw the tattered, flannel shirt at her.

"Gross! You're awful." Sailor blocked the shirt and shoved Forest, which knocked him to the floor.

While the two of them duked it out, I turned to

the first page in the journal and shined my light on it. "Listen to this." I began reading:

June 1st, 1939. Started with the WPA at Point Beach. Met up with the crew in Manitowoc. Jobs are scarce. Only a fool would turn down the work.

*Fifteen of us boarded a truck with parallel planks across the back — cattle wagon-style. The truck bounced down the two-lane dirt road, passing corn-fields, scrawny pines and milk thistle along the way.
A few of the guys seemed to know each other. A bois-terous crew. I steered clear of them. Always been a loner.*

"Wow, so this guy actually worked here!" Sailor exclaimed.

I skipped over the next few pages, when a torn-out picture from a magazine caught my eye. It was a picture of a bunker.

I continued to read aloud:

Saw an article about a WWI German bunker. Oppor-tunity knocked when a small group of us hauled gar-bage to the junkyard. Someone left a pile of sheet met-al. I had to talk the others into letting me take it. That, along with some of the hand-cut stones we used for the rangers' lodge would do nicely for a hideaway. Lord knows I could use the privacy.

"Cool!" I looked up. "Hey, that might explain why I felt like someone was watching me earlier. Maybe there's something valuable hidden in here!"

Forest sat down at the table and began finishing the solitaire game. "Looks like we might have another mystery on our hands. We need to come back with some matches for that kerosene lamp and take a good look around."

As I closed the book, something fell out. It was a poem, handwritten on a tattered piece of paper with a feather sketched at the top.

The haunting tale of the red man
Whispers and weaves through the reeds
And there the Great Spirit travails
For all of the white man's misdeeds.

Where the natives have languished and lingered
Before their great trail of tears
You can still hear their voices cry out
From the earth, lo, for all of these years.

Bang the drum where their voices now carry
Light a fire to signal on high
The Great Spirit still grieves for the red man
If you listen, you might hear Him cry.

Forest narrowed his eyes. "What's the big idea? We find this really cool bunker, and now we're supposed to listen to all this boring junk that some lumberjack poet wrote in his book?"

He got up and stretched. "Lame deck of cards. The ace of spades is missing. No wonder the caveman didn't finish the game."

"Hang on a minute and look at this!" I removed a photograph sticking out from underneath the cover sleeve. The faded, black and white picture was of an elderly Native American woman. I turned the picture over. "On the back it says 'Wawetseka.' Huh. I wonder who she is?"

"She's Wawetseka," Sailor said.

Forest rolled his eyes at her.

"There's a lot more written in here. I'll read it later when you're not around. I wouldn't want to bore you." I tucked the book into my backpack.

"Let's get out of here. This place is giving me the creeps." Sailor nervously rubbed her arms.

One by one, we made our way back up the stairs.

Forest closed the hatch while I gathered nearby leaves and branches to cover the bunker, when something caught my eye. "Hey, guys, I see footprints here!"

Forest and Sailor looked in the direction I was pointing to. A set of large boot prints were imprinted in the dirt nearby, heading out toward the main trail. I'm sure we all wondered the same thing—who else knew about this bunker?

We got back to Forest and Sailor's campsite just in time for supper. GB was stacking logs into the fire pit. Judging from his outfit, he was trying to impress Windsong. A wide-brimmed canvas hat covered his bald head; his jeans were tucked into knee-high moccasins.

"Hi kids! You're just in time for dinner. Grab a seat." Windsong set a plate of raisins and cashews on the table.

The Thai food looked edible. I loaded my plate

with rice and pineapples. Windsong is a vegan, so I didn't dare ask if there was shrimp in the deal.

After we all had our fill, we retired to the campfire. I really liked their site. It was private, and the woods behind the split-rail cedar fence offered a peaceful backdrop.

"So, what have you kids been up to?" Windsong pulled up a chair next to me.

"Not much. We biked on Ridges Trail."

"Dreamy!" she replied, sipping from her glass of mint tea.

GB raised an eyebrow. "I'm surprised Dominic went anywhere after the nightmare he had last night."

"I read a book on interpreting dreams not too long ago. Would you like to tell me about it?" Windsong asked.

I stared into the flickering flames for a moment.

"Okay," I finally relented, "but I really don't see how you can help."

I told her the dream about the bear chasing me through the woods, the metal trunk with the rusty arrow and the blue flowers.

"Interesting, given that there actually was a bear sighting. And to me, the trunk speaks of hidden things, and the rusty arrow … hmm … something that was around a long time, perhaps."

I leaned in closer to the crackling fire.

"The blue flowers could be Smurfs—just sayin'," Forest added.

A glowing chunk of wood shot out of the fire pit, headed straight for Sailor, which sent her running in the opposite direction. So much for her marshmallow. It trickled like white lava into the flames.

GB pulled his chair closer. "Dominic, I don't want you to worry about this. First of all, not every dream necessarily has meaning. And second, the Lord doesn't give us more than we can handle. So, if something strange and mysterious turns up at Point Beach, I want you to promise you'll tell me about it."

Sailor jumped to her feet. "Something bad happened already! A giant tarantula—"

"Sailor!" Forest shot her a warning look. "It

wasn't a tarantula; it was a daddy longlegs. This isn't the Motel 6, you know. We're in the woods. They're everywhere."

I was glad the subject was changed. There was no way I could tell GB about the bunker. Bad enough there was a bear on the loose.

CHAPTER 4

The next morning, Forest, Sailor and I biked to the nature center for the campground meeting. A historical marker stood just outside the building. I had seen it before but hadn't paid too much attention.

I walked over to the marker. "Hold up, guys. It's about the WPA crew. Maybe it could provide another clue about Ray and what he was doing here."

Forest and Sailor looked over my shoulder, reading the information.

"Restoring the Land Renewed Their Spirit," was the headline. The sign described the development of Point Beach State Forest through the WPA project. The "Works Progress Administration," was a government initiative to help unemployed workers during the Great Depression.

Several pictures showed hardworking men using shovels, picks, and saws. Part of their job was to build the lodge, clear roads, cut stones, and plant trees.

"Pretty cool!" Forest said. "So, this was some of the work Ray did at Point Beach."

"Yeah. I read some more of his journal last night. It explains a few things, but I'll have to show you after the meeting."

Cling. Clang. Clong. A loud racket drummed in our ears. We turned around to see Ranger Rick, banging pots and pans together.

"Is it time for lunch, Ranger?" Forest teased.

"Well, if it isn't 'Nimrod' and the two 'Illi-annoyers.' You won't be such wise crackers when you're being chased by a hungry bear," Ranger Rick scoffed.

Here we go again.

"I've been securing the area, so that bear doesn't make Point Beach part of its habitat." Ranger Rick fumbled to push his hat back with his hands full of pans. "Now, quit your dilly-dallying and get inside. Don't you know the meeting is about to start?"

"Yes sir," I said.

We went inside. GB and Windsong were sitting next to the Buckleys. We found three empty chairs in a row behind them.

"Oh, if it isn't the three famous detectives who put Point Beach on the map!" Mrs. Buckley swept her hand in our direction.

Ranger Rick glared at us from across the room. "Take a seat. I was just about to make an important announcement."

He set down his kitchen jamboree on a table and cleared his throat.

"Now, folks, it looks like we have a serious problem here at the campground. Someone reported that a bear tried to run off with their picnic basket yesterday."

Several people gasped, including Sailor, who nearly swallowed her gum.

"Now, now. Don't let your imagination run wild. My partner, Sally, will distribute some pamphlets on your way out."

He nodded in the direction of the plump, bru-

nette ranger standing by the doorway. She smiled
bashfully.

He opened one up and began reading it.

"If you see a bear but he doesn't see you …

Stay calm. Do not announce your presence.

Keep your distance. Do not panic.

Go back the way you came. Do not run.

Move downwind, not upwind."

He turned to the next page: "Now, if you see a
bear and he sees you:

Speak in a low tone. Do not shout.

Wave your arms slowly to make yourself look
big." He circled his arms to demonstrate.

Forest leaned over and whispered into my ear,
"If he flaps his arms any faster, he'll be able to fly over
the bear."

I tried not to chuckle.

The ranger continued:

"Retreat calmly and slowly. Do not run."

He closed the page "One last thing. If the bear
follows you or charges, stop and stand your ground."

A burly, muscular man with thick, red hair and a bristly beard stood up. "Conroy here. Wade Conroy." He turned to the crowd. "What the ranger said is true. If you act afraid of the bear, he will have his way with you."

Ranger Rick's face flushed. Looked like the steam engine was about to blow.

"Now, listen here, Cowboy. Nobody asked you for your opinion. As the ranger of this park, I'm the only one with the authority to give these directions." He patted his badge.

The guy who called himself Conroy held up his hands. "Ah, no offense, Ranger. And it's 'Conroy,' not 'Cowboy.' I'm a professional hunter. I come from a family of hunters. Not only do I hunt and kill wild animals, I'm a certified taxidermist"—he pointed to a stuffed bear and a stuffed racoon in the room— "so I know what I'm talking about."

He felt around in his front shirt pocket. "Here's my card, in case you're interested in my services."

Ranger Rick shoved the business card back at

him. "Put that marketing propaganda away. The information we're disseminating here is how to flee from a bear, not how to kill and stuff one."

Sally hurried over, radio in hand, her face drawn out and pale. "Excuse me, Ranger Rick, but I've just been alerted. We have a — *situation* — at the lodge."

On that note, Ranger Rick abruptly ended the meeting. He ushered everyone out the door, with Sally handing out the safety guides.

"I wonder what that's all about?" I said to Forest and Sailor.

"Nimrod," Ranger Rick eyed me, "I don't want any trouble from you. Don't go getting any big ideas that you're going to hunt down the bear and save the campground. That's my job."

Forest looked like he was about to make a smart-aleck comment, so I shoved him toward the door.

"Hey, I think that guy dropped something." Forest bent down, grabbed the business card off the floor, and began reading it out loud.

"Catchy slogan." He jammed the card into his pocket.

"Well, that was certainly an interesting meeting." GB and Windsong joined us.

"We all need to keep these guides on bear encounters in our back pockets. But God willing, we won't have to deal with that." GB shook his head.

"Rangers and guns and bears, oh my!" Windsong shuddered at the thought, then turned to GB. "How about we take a walk on the beach, Bobby? I would love to add to my sea glass collection."

"Sounds good to me." He turned to us. "Maybe you kids want to spend some time rebuilding your fort?"

"Aren't we getting a little too old for that?" I used to look forward to hanging out in our driftwood hide-away with Forest and Sailor, hashing out our next great mystery that needed solving. But now we had a new fort that our grandparents knew nothing about.

He shook his finger at us. "You kids stay out of trouble, you hear?"

"No problem, GB. We're actually planning on having a snack at our campsite anyway," I said.

"We are?" Sailor's eyes lit up.

I shot her down with a stink eye. "Yeah, remember? My mom made, um, cookies."

"Oh … yeah." She scratched her head, looking completely and thoroughly baffled.

"I see Nimrod made it another year." Forest shook his head in amusement as we walked inside.

I put up with his abuse every summer, getting teased endlessly for GB's idea of a cheap vacation. Nimrod was as old as the lumberjack's bunker. Smelled like it, too.

"How about those cookies you promised?" Forest took a seat at the small Formica table. I reached into the cabinet where GB kept the snacks, grabbing the package of cookies and a bag of cheese popcorn.

"Delicious." Sailor helped herself to a cookie.

"So, Dominic, what did you find out about that beatnik poet?" Forest reached for a handful of popcorn.

I took a seat next to them, grabbing the journal from the nearby shelf. "GB insisted on turning in early last night because of this morning's meeting, and there was nothing for me to do but read in the dark with my flashlight." I opened the book.

"Most of it is about the government work project. How the lumberjacks from Manitowoc were chopping down trees and stuff and building the roads here. Ray worked on the crew that built the rangers' lodge."

"Did you find out who the woman was?" Sailor asked.

"She was Ray's great-grandmother from the Potawatomi tribe. He seemed pretty impressed with their culture. and wrote a lot about it. His mom even gave him a nickname when he was little—Running Bear."

"I wanna see what he wrote!" Sailor reached for the journal, sending a few popcorn pieces flying as she leaned over the table.

"Settle down, Sailor!" Forest glared at her. "Why don't you go get an Orange Crush."

"I don't *want* an Orange Crush," she whined.

"Who said it was for you?" Forest grabbed the book out of her hands and began flipping through it.

"Hey, Dominic. Did you see this?" He opened the book to a section that had a gap, as if the page had been ripped out.

"Yeah, I was getting to that. Read what Ray says on the page before it."

Forest turned back the page, and read the entry:

Chet really got my goat today. He's been snooping around, looking for the artifact. I know his kind. Nothing is sacred to him. I had to keep the item safe.
I know he's been hanging around the bunker. I saw his footprints. On the chance that anything happens to me, I drew a map that leads to the hiding place.

"Wow!" Sailor sat back. "So, it's possible that something valuable is hidden right here at Point Beach!"

CHAPTER 5

"What's the point of getting excited?" Forest tossed the book aside. "The map's gone. No chance we're ever going to find it now."

I walked over to GB's junk drawer, next to the sink. "A good detective knows where to look for clues."

"Where? In an old dude's antique camper?" Forest sneered.

"I'm looking for a pencil. Did it ever occur to you that we might be able to make an imprint of the missing page?" I pushed aside a handful of rubber bands, paper clips, shoelaces and an old toothbrush, but couldn't find anything to write with, not even a crayon. I did find a book of matches, however, which I stuffed into my pocket.

"Do you have a pencil at your campsite?"

Forest and Sailor looked at each other.

"I don't think we used pencils since we were in kindergarten," Forest said, "and the only tool Windsong would have is a knitting needle."

"Okay. Let's go to the office." I put the journal into my backpack, and we headed out.

As we made our way past the rangers' lodge, a flickering of red and blue lights caught our attention. I hit the brakes on my bike, which nearly caused Sailor to crash into me.

"Holy schnikes!" Forest pulled up alongside us. "What's going on?"

Ranger Rick was barking orders to a pair of deputies and a K9 unit. Glass shards were scattered around a basement window.

"Maybe we can get some information at the office." I took off on my bike, with Forest and Sailor following close behind.

The parking lot was full. Probably lots of campers had the same questions we did. We made our way inside.

Ranger Sally was addressing the crowd. "I know

you're all wondering about the commotion at the rangers' lodge. All I can tell you for now, is that there was a break-in sometime during this morning's meeting."

A rumbling of voices arose in the room. A red-haired woman standing next to a tall, gangly man swiftly picked up her toddler, who had been clinging to her legs. An elderly man in a checkered shirt and a ponytail was standing behind them, peering out the window in the direction of the lodge.

The toddler reached out his hand and yanked on the old guy's ponytail. The man smiled at the boy, then returned his attention to the scene at the rangers' lodge. Other gawkers were trying to see out the window, too.

"Folks, please keep it down. Ranger Rick has everything under control." At the mention of the ranger, she blushed, flipping back her hair. "Now, remain calm and go about your day." And with that, she walked over to the drive-thru window to assist a camper who had just pulled in with an RV.

"Let's head out." I made my way to the door.

"Wait. What about the pencil?" Forest asked.

"Got it. No one was paying attention, so I resorted to helping myself from the desk."

"So, what do you make of the robbery?" Sailor asked as we sat down at a picnic table outside the office. She was twirling her pigtails, which usually indicated she was scared as a rabbit.

"First off, no one said anything was stolen. Besides, what would there even be to steal in there?" I ripped a piece of paper from my notebook, placing it over the journal entry that was behind the missing page.

"Maybe one of the rangers has a valuable coin collection," Forest said.

"I suppose that's possible. But the bigger question is, does this have anything to do with what Ray was hiding? Think about it … he worked on the crew that built the rangers' lodge. That would be a logical hiding place."

"Well, yeah. But that's a big leap. It was more than a few years ago when that happened."

"Well, lookie, lookie!" Bert Buckley came rumbling up in his golf cart, decked out in a plaid shirt, jean overalls and a straw hat.

I can't say I was thrilled to see him. We were just about to uncover a major clue in the case.

"Did you kids hear about the break-in?" He walked up to the picnic table and propped his foot up on the bench; a toothpick hanging from the corner of his mouth.

"Yes, and we heard about the bear, too." Sailor leaned forward on her elbows. "Mr. Buckley, have you seen the bear?"

Bert started to speak, then gagged as the toothpick got lodged between his lip and the roof of his mouth. After a near puncture wound, he managed to flip it back out.

"Well, little lady, I've seen plenty of bears in my lifetime, but not in this neck of the woods. I've seen racoons, chipmunks, squirrels, toads, rabbits, badgers, … all kinds of birds …" He stared off into space.

Time was slipping away. If only I could think of a po-

lite way to get Bert to take off.

"Skunks, rabbits, turtles, foxes, oh, and that pig that was camping here last summer."

"You shouldn't refer to the campers as pigs," Forest retorted with a crooked grin.

Windsong would have pulled his ears if she heard the insolence.

Bert didn't seem to appreciate that last comment. He rolled up his sleeves and leaned in toward Forest. "I suggest you kids don't get into any mischief. There's enough going on here to keep the law busy. Any interference on your part would look bad for you."

"Well, sir, if it looks bad for me, it makes Dominic look bad. And if Dominic looks bad, it looks bad for Sailor, so … let's just focus on Sailor."

Hehe. I could tell Bert's head was spinning. Forest has that effect on people.

"It's too bad the crooks got a clean break. Years ago, I came up with a plan for a time such as this." He puffed out his chest. "The plan was to petition the county to put cameras in the park."

"Really?" I was starting to feel a thread of hope.

"Sure did. Looking back, I wish I had followed through on that plan." He shook his head.

"Well, I best be heading back to the campsite. Mrs. Buckley needs my help in stringing up the pink flamingo lights I bought in Two Rivers." He lumbered back to the golf cart, waved and drove out of sight.

"It's about time! I thought he'd never leave," Forest moaned.

I turned to the last page of the journal, placing my blank sheet of paper over the top of it. I rubbed across the page with the rough edge of the pencil until a pattern began to emerge.

CHAPTER 6

It worked!

The faint outline of an oblong, two-story building showed up beneath the pencil rubbing. On the inside there was a distinct line leading into a large room with an arrow pointing to a spot near the south wall. A sentence in a strange language appeared beneath it:

"Giin waa mikan zagaswe'idiwag opwaagan dazhi makwa."

I read the words out loud, but they sounded like gibberish. "I have no clue what that means."

"Maybe some of the lettering from the other pages transferred onto this one?" Sailor suggested.

"Let's get back to that later." I stared at the paper once more. "Judging by the doors and windows, if I didn't know any better, I'd say the missing page was a sketch of the rangers' lodge!" Excitement tingled down my spine. "The break-in can't be a coincidence. Someone else tore out the map and stole the hidden artifact."

"Just because someone found this map and broke into the lodge, that doesn't mean they found what they were looking for." Forest grabbed the map out of my hands. "We'll need to see for ourselves."

I surveyed the lodge, situated alongside the main road of the campground. The police entourage had dissipated, and Ranger Rick's truck was absent from his usual spot in front of the garage door.

"Unfortunately, the room we need to investigate has all the shades drawn. Someone will need to get inside," I said.

"Hey, I think I see that nice ranger lady over there. We could ask her if we can look for clues," Sailor suggested.

"That's one idea, but she doesn't even know us, and what if Ranger Rick shows up?" I watched Sally carry a few boxes out of the lodge and load them onto the back of an ATV.

"I'm sure you'll think of something. Once you're inside, Sailor and I will do the rest. Let's go. Chop.

Chop." Forest shoved me off the picnic table bench.

This could only mean trouble.

We approached the lodge, taking a few steps along the chiseled stone exterior of the building toward where Sally was working.

"Can I help you kids with something?" Sally walked over with a rosy-cheeked smile.

"Oh, yes please!" Forest stepped forward. "My friend Dominic, here, needs to use the bathroom *really* bad." He pointed at me.

I wanted to give him a swift kick in the shin but decided to go along with the plan. "Can I please use the bathroom? It's an emergency!" I did my most convincing potty-dance to help with the persuasion.

"Well, it looks like you're not going to make it much longer," Sally chuckled. "Run inside, take the first door to the right and head straight to the back."

"Thanks!" I bolted through the front door, hoping Forest and Sailor would keep her busy long enough for me to find what we were looking for.

I immediately headed into the room marked on

Ray's diagram. It was pitch dark with the shades closed until I turned on the light switch. At first glance, the place looked like it needed some major updates, with all the shaggy carpeting, dark paneled walls, and peeling paint.

There were a dozen chairs set up around a long table, covered in dust. A metal rack filled with ranger uniforms was shoved in the corner next to a stack of boxes piled along a wall.

Using the sketch to guide me, I went right to the exact place where the arrow was pointing, but the spot was completely bare. All I could see was a patch of matted carpeting with a faded imprint on the wall behind it.

"We're too late. There's nothing here," I mumbled to myself while snapping a few pictures using my cell phone.

Over by the clothes rack I found a row of metal file cabinets that I hadn't noticed at first. I opened the bottom drawer that was labeled "Expense reports and zoning permits." Each file was classified by year, and to my surprise, one of them went all the way back to 1939. *This might be useful.*

After pulling the file from the drawer, I quickly spread the documents out onto the long table and took a picture of each one. My nerves were telling me I needed to hurry. Time was short before Sally would get suspicious.

I put the file away, checking that everything was back in place. Then I took a quick run through the rest of the building to make sure I didn't miss anything. On my way out, I dashed into the bathroom and "flushed" before rejoining the others.

"Thanks again. I feel much better." I interrupted Sally who was in a conversation with Forest and Sailor—probably discussing the weather. "I noticed you're moving some boxes. Where's all that stuff going?"

"To the donation bin. The lodge is in the process of getting cleared out for renovations. All that's left are a few things that accumulated over the past seventy years," Sally said. "Fortunately, the valuables were put into storage before the break-in."

"Whew, that *is* good news," I agreed, but our investigation was cut short. Coming up the drive was Ranger Rick in his truck, full steam ahead.

"Okay, well then … have a great day." Forest turned to leave. Sailor and I were about to follow.

"Hold up, buttercup." Sally stood in front of us. "I bet I know who you kids are. You're those young private eyes the Buckley's were telling me about. Aren't you?"

We looked at each other, not sure if we should answer her or make a break for it.

"Of course you are. No need to be humble." Sally gave us a wink.

It was too late. Ranger Rick parked his truck and barged over.

"Every time I turn around, you three are up to something." He glared at us.

Sally put her hand on my shoulder. "This gentleman just had to go and pay the water bill, so I let him inside, but only for a minute," she assured him.

Ranger Rick gave me the evil-eye. "Alright, buster. You know this is a crime scene, and I can't have you tampering with evidence."

"All he did was use some toilet paper—you call that evidence?" Forest argued.

"Don't push my buttons, Illinoyance." Ranger Rick put his hands on his hips. "I better take a look around, just to be sure." He climbed the front step and opened the door to the lodge.

"My boss sure has a way with words, but underneath that rough exterior, there's a heart of gold. I just know it." Sally batted her eyelashes before following him inside.

"More like, 'heart of stone.' Man, is she in for a rude awakening," Forest grumbled.

"So are we, if we don't get out of here," I said. "Let's go."

"So … what did you find inside the lodge?" Sailor asked once we reached the road leading back to the campground.

"It's just a big house, basically. There's a kitchen, TV room with a bar and a couple of bathrooms and bedrooms. The place was empty except for a few things piled in the office. Take a look for yourself." I showed her the pictures on my phone.

"Okay, but did you find anything to do with the artifact?" Forest rephrased the question.

"Not really. Either the burglar took whatever Ray was hiding, or the artifact was moved for renovations. I guess we're too late."

"What's this list of names for?" Sailor scrolled down and enlarged one of my screen shots from the file documents.

"I don't know. I was just looking for anything that might date back to that year in Ray's journal."

Forest grabbed the phone from Sailor. "Wow, Dominic, I'm impressed. You found a list of all the WPA lumberjacks who worked at Point Beach. Guess whose name is at the top?"

"Ray Anderson?" I could only hope.

"Yep! And that makes me wonder if that Chet guy is on here, too." Forest ran his finger down the screen. In about two seconds he announced, "Jackpot!"

"Awesome!" Sailor yelled. "We found a clue."

"More than a clue—we found a suspect." Forest stared at the screen. "Chet's last name is *Conroy*."

CHAPTER 7

"Chet Conroy? I knew that name sounded familiar." I reached for the bag of bread and the jar of peanut butter on the picnic table at our campsite.

"Yeah, he's gotta be related to Wade Conroy, the taxidermist who wanted to help Ranger Rick hunt for the bear," Forest said.

I handed him a sandwich. Sailor declined.

"No thanks, Dominic. All I can think about is that gross taxidermy book back at the bunker." She turned up her nose.

"Oh, yeah. I almost forgot about that." Forest raised his eyebrows. "That's another clue."

I took a big bite of PB&J. My brain was racing through the series of events. "Wait a minute, guys. We have a problem."

"Come on, Dominic. The sun's shining, it's a beautiful day—don't try to ruin it now." Forest reached for a can of cola and took a big bite of his sandwich.

"If Wade Conroy was at the meeting, then how could he be at the lodge at the same time?" I slumped in my seat until a small animal ran up to me like a flash of lightning, eating the sandwich right out of my hand.

"Sprinkles, behave yourself!" Mrs. Buckley retracted the long leash, keeping Sprinkles at bay from devouring the rest of our lunch.

"Aren't you just the cutest little thing." Sailor ruffled the poodle's fuzzy ears.

Sprinkles was wearing a fluorescent orange vest. I should've seen her coming a mile away.

"Sprinky needs to wear this vest for protection. I don't want my wittle-precious-poopsie to be used for target practice." Mrs. Buckley held her hand to her forehead. "Until that bear gets rounded up, I don't think I'll ever feel safe."

Sprinkles began to bark at something behind our campsite. Mrs. B. looked as though she was about to have a full-blown panic attack, but it was only our grandparents coming over the ridge.

"Kids, look what we found!" Windsong outstretched her arm, palm closed. She opened her grasp, revealing a smooth, polished stone, chiseled into the shape of an arrowhead.

"Isn't it great!" GB's eyes grew wide with anticipation as we passed it around.

"Cool. Where'd you find it?" Sailor asked.

"In a washout where Molash Creek runs into Lake Michigan," Windsong explained. "I looked down and there it was—right at my feet."

"You know that taxidermist, Wade Conroy, from Whitelaw?" Mrs. Buckley interrupted. "I was talking to him before the meeting. Turns out he's a collector. I bet he could tell you all about it."

Interesting …

"Maybe we should check it out. I've been to Whitelaw before. It's not too far from here," GB said.

"He showed me a brochure about his taxidermy shop. You kids would enjoy it. The way they have it decorated, it's almost like a museum." Mrs. Buckley nodded with a smile, revealing her coffee-stained teeth.

"I wanna go!" Sailor yelled.

"Yeah, me too! This would be a good history lesson for us. It's a museum!"

Forest said the magic words. Windsong nodded. "All right, I suppose there's no harm in it."

"Great." GB held his elbow toward her to hook her arm in. "We should head out before it gets dark. Let's go kids!"

The short drive into Whitelaw led us to a quaint village shop, right on the main road leading through town. A large orange and brown neon sign that read, "Conroy Taxidermy and Pawn Shop," hung crooked in the front window; a small "OPEN" sign tacked beneath it.

"Pawn shop?" Windsong objected. "What are we getting ourselves into?"

"Now, now. Let's just see what's going on here."

GB walked up to the door. As he pulled on the handle, a few bells rang in the doorway announcing our arrival.

We stepped inside, expecting to find mounts on the walls of deer, bears, and trophy fish. Instead, there were several small tables with what looked like giant fish tanks on top of them. Small taxidermy animals dressed in clothing were set up inside. Each one was placed in human-like positions.

Inside the first display was a diorama of two squirrels in a fishing boat, just their size. They each wore fishing caps and vests with lures hooked to them. The boat rested on a clear, plastic platform, made to look like water.

"This is hilarious, check it out!" I said to Forest.

Each squirrel was pulling on their fishing pole, but the lines were tangled beneath the boat. There were three taxidermy fish looking up at the squirrels, their lips shaped as though they were laughing.

"Ha, ha. Those squirrels won't catch much that way." Forest leaned up to the display.

"Well, hello there."

We looked up just as Wade Conroy walked in from a side room. He was wearing glasses, with a full-length plastic apron and white gloves on his hands.

"Can I help you with anything?" He smiled at us as he peeled the vinyl from each finger before removing the gloves with a slap of elastic.

"Yes, actually, a friend of ours told us about your taxidermy shop, but we had no idea that this was the kind of work you do." Windsong shuddered as she glanced around the room.

Given that she was a vegan, I'm sure she wasn't "digging" this place.

"These certainly are one of a kind," GB admitted. "You have lots of talent."

"Why, thank you," he replied. "I gather all sorts of things to put into my work, thanks to all the roadkill on Highway 10."

"Eww, is he serious?" Sailor murmured.

"By chance, would you know anything about the arrowhead I found?" Windsong reached into her purse and pulled out a plastic baggie.

Wade leaned in for a closer look.

"Very nice. I'm not sure how much of an expert I am, but I'd say it's made from flint. The blade is ovate with a beveled edge, as you can see here." He ran a finger along the serrated side. "They sell quite a few of these at the pawn shop, but I don't run that half of the family business."

"Well, mine's not for sale." Windsong slipped the arrowhead back into her pocket.

"No problem. Would you like to see the ones that I have in my collection?"

"That would be great!" I beamed.

When Wade led us into the side room, the taxidermy shop started to look more like I imagined. Half-open drawers filled with supplies supported a counter containing animal pelts and feathers. Various-sized scissors, needles, and scalpels hung from pegs.

"The taxidermy shop keeps me pretty busy, but what I really enjoy is creating works of art." He stood in front of a glass case on the wall. A variety of arrowheads were arranged in colorful patterns and designs, secured to a red velvet backdrop.

"Groovy." Windsong stared, wide-eyed. "Where did they all come from?"

"Point Beach," he said.

Forest and Sailor locked eyes with me after Wade made reference to Point Beach — *the scene of the crime.*

"Funny, that's where we're camping this weekend," GB told him. "We found the arrowhead by Molash Creek."

"My family used to own property near there. Great for hunting. It was also a favorite place of the Potawatomi and Ottawa who lived along the lakeshore long before we did."

"Yes, I believe Rawley Point was closely named after Peter Rowley, one of the first settlers who set up a trading post with the tribes there," GB said.

Wade nodded. "They lived the way nature intended. They hunted ... used the animal pelts for clothing and fallen trees for firewood to stay warm in the brutal cold winters. Even made birch canoes to fish on the rivers and lakes in the summers."

"They sure lived differently than us," Sailor said.

"There's a few things we could all learn from their culture." Wade looked at his wristwatch. "I suppose I shouldn't keep you, and I do have a deadline to fulfill. I'm trying to finish my latest masterpiece to exhibit at the Lumberjack World Championship."

"Oh, could we see it please?" Sailor clasped her hands.

"Sure, stop and take a peek on your way out. It's the one with a sheet over it."

After we said goodbye, Wade returned to his work. We went back through the main shop, stopping by the display tucked away in the corner. GB removed the sheet that covered it so that we could look inside.

A badger and a weasel were playing poker at a table. The badger was betting all his chips but didn't see that the weasel had a carrot behind his back. He was slipping it to a rabbit, dressed in an overcoat, in exchange for an ace card.

"Say, look at that Green Bay Packer ace card! I

used to have a deck of cards just like that back in the day." GB looked like a kid in a candy store.

Forest nudged me in the ribs. He was pointing at the ace card.

Hmmm. Where have I seen that before?

CHAPTER 8

We all piled into GB's truck and headed down Main Street. Out of curiosity, I began looking for squirrels that never made it across the road.

"Well, I have to say, I did not like that animal circus one bit." Windsong folded her arms. "Those creatures are God's trophies, not ours."

"It did seem kind of creepy," Forest agreed. "This big bear hunter guy arranges little squirrels and rodents and things like they're in a dollhouse."

"I thought they were cute." Sailor giggled.

Off to the right, a corner bar with flashy lights caught Windsong's attention.

"Oh, look GB! Gill's Bar & Grill is having a fish fry. I could go for a salad, but I know you boys like your fish. We could eat here and then I won't have to cook tonight. What do you think?"

"Yesss!" Forest, Sailor and I yelled. Anything

was better than Windsong's cooking. And I mean any-thing.

GB seemed more than happy to oblige. He pulled the truck into the parking lot.

"Looks like the restaurant is packed to the 'gills," Forest joked.

Luckily, we found an open table. After the waitress took our order and collected our menus, I glanced toward the counter. Was I seeing double? The husky, bearded redhead sitting on the bar stool looked just like Wade Conroy.

I motioned for Forest and Sailor to take a look. They glanced in his direction. The saltshaker Forest had been playing with rolled to the floor.

"How did he get here so fast? He was in the taxidermy shop when we left."

"Weird," Sailor agreed.

Only one way to solve this mystery. I walked up to the counter.

"Hi, Mr. Conroy."

"Oh, hi kid. I'm kinda busy here. Did you need

something?" He was looking seriously annoyed.

My face turned as red as the bottle of ketchup on the counter. "Oh, uh, nothing. Just wondering how you got here so quick. You know, from your shop."

Without another word, he turned back to the bartender, handing him the exact change for his to-go order. He picked up the package of greasy burgers, and I went back to the table for mine.

That was awkward.

The next morning, I called Forest on my walkie-talkie. I hoped that he kept the one I gave him close by. As luck would have it, he did.

"Dominator to Woody … come in." (I'm Dominator, Forest is Woody. Our code names from a previous mystery in the park.)

Kwttchhh … "Woody here. What's up?"

"Meet me at our place in 0900 hours."

"Will do. Over and out."

I wolfed down a bowl of Frosted Flakes before GB had a chance to even think about cooking grits, or any other weird vegetable dish. After I slipped on my tennis shoes, I took a quick look in the mirror. Not too shabby. All I needed to do was run a wet comb through my hair.

I brushed my bangs to one side like how Forest wears his, but that didn't seem to suit me. Besides, I like being able to see. I just spiked it up as usual and headed outside.

"See you later, GB!"

He looked up from his bear-hunting book. "Hold up there, Dominic. Where are you off to?"

"I'm going to hang out with Forest and Sailor."

"That's fine. Windsong and I are going back to the beach to look for sea glass again. She's got it in her head to make a wind chime. I'll leave out some cheese and fruit in case you come back hungry."

As I rode my bike to the bunker, I mulled over the strange events from the day before. Wade had acted like he didn't even remember me. Worse, Dr. Jekyll had turned into Mr. Hyde. How could he be nice one minute and nasty the next?

When I neared the camp host site, I noticed Bert and Sadie were sitting by the fire pit with Sprinkles lying in her doggie bed next to them. I started pedaling faster, hoping they wouldn't see me.

"Yoo hoo! Danny!"

Dang it.

I pulled up alongside them.

"Have you kids seen the bear yet? Ranger Rick just stopped by. Someone saw it by Molash Creek. He's on his way in that direction." Bert pointed down Ridges Trail.

"We haven't seen the bear," I said. "But we'll be careful."

"Well, see that you do!" Sadie shook her finger at me. "The last thing we need around here is for that bear to get his paws on you."

"What's that you say about a bear claw?" Bert licked his lips.

Sadie hit him over the head with a fly swatter. "I

said, 'Don't-let-the-bear-get-his-paws-on-you,'" she yelled into his good ear. "I'm not talking about donuts."

While they were distracted, I pedaled off, arriving at the bunker at the same time Forest and Sailor did. We parked our bikes by a nearby tree and walked over.

Forest pulled the hatch open and started making the descent down the steps. Sailor went down next. There must not have been any spiders, because she was in pretty quickly.

My turn.

As I reached the last rung, I heard a blood-curdling scream that was so loud, it could have woken the dead.

Sailor was staring at the bed. Someone was lying in it. A fly was buzzing around the body, sort of like a vulture does when it's hovering over roadkill. The dark figure started moving—a gnarled hand reached up to swat the fly away.

I guess her scream had the intended effect, because the man sat up. It was the same elderly guy I saw in the office yesterday.

"What's going on?" He blinked a few times before covering his eyes.

I realized my flashlight was pointed at him. I turned it off. "Sorry, Sir. We found this bunker and didn't know anyone still lived here."

"No one lives here. At least not anymore." He studied the three of us. "I know what you're doing here. You're looking for my map."

I couldn't believe it. Ray was alive!

CHAPTER 9

"Don't look so surprised. I've been hanging around the bunker and couldn't help but overhear your conversations. You took my journal … and my map."

"Sir, can we please explain?" Forest offered. "We didn't mean any harm."

I stepped forward. "We did take your journal. Sorry about that. But we didn't take your map. Someone beat us to it."

"It was Chet. No-good lumberjack. He's been pestering me for some time now." He stood then, looking confused at his surroundings.

"Wait a minute, you wrote that Chet was bothering you, but that was over eighty years ago," Forest interjected.

Ray cleared his throat. "Yes, of course. I know that." He walked over to the kerosene lamp, striking a match to the wick. The amber light rippled across the walls, casting an eerie glow. "Why don't we introduce ourselves? Obviously, I'm Ray. Who might you be?"

"I'm Dominic, and these are my friends, Forest and Sailor."

"Now, those are names you don't hear every day." Ray sat back.

I had to give him credit. In his red-checkered shirt, jeans and ponytail, he still looked like a lumberjack. But he was also soft-spoken and gentle, like a poet.

"We camp here every summer, and even solved a few mysteries at this park," Forest said.

"Yes, that's why we were so interested when we read in your journal about the artifact that you hid." Sailor smiled shyly. "Can you tell us where it is?"

"I wish it was that simple. Chet clobbered me over the head which resulted in amnesia for all these years. He tried to convince everyone it was a 'logging accident,' but that didn't sit right with me—something seemed wrong with his story."

"How did you find your way back here if you

couldn't remember anything?" I asked.

"It was only recently that my memory started to return. The Herald Times Reporter wrote an article about me when they heard I was celebrating my 100th birthday. Talking about my job with the WPA helped me remember things."

"You're a hundred?" Sailor's eyes popped.

Ray chuckled. "Guess being a lumberjack kept me in good shape all these years." He reached into his pocket for the article and set it on the table, smoothing his hand over the wrinkles. Forest leaned in to take a look.

"Trouble is," Ray continued, "my memory isn't fully back yet. I remember Point Beach, and this bunker, and I even remember the journal." He scratched his head. "But gee willikers, I can't remember where I hid the peace pipe."

At the mention of the peace pipe, I got excited. "So *that's* what the artifact is. We were wondering about that."

Ray rubbed the back of his neck. "That pipe belonged to Chief Waumegesako, or Chief Mexico, as the white settlers liked to call him. He was well-loved and respected in the community and played an important role in the signing of several treaties for Green Bay and Chicago, among other cities during the 20s and 30s. My great-grandmother, Wawetseka, lived among his tribe."

"We saw her picture. She's very pretty." Sailor's eyes lit up.

"Her name actually means 'pretty woman' in the Potawatomi language," he said.

"Is that how you ended up with the pipe?" I didn't remember anything in the journal about it.

The lines on Ray's face deepened. "It was reported that robbers stole it a few years after the chief died. It was never recovered, until one day Chet left his work bag behind. When I grabbed it to return to him, lo and behold, something fell out. I immediately recognized it was Chief Mexico's peace pipe! In that moment, I knew I had to keep it safely hidden until I could notify the proper tribal committee."

"Wow! That was some find. I bet you were really excited!" Forest interrupted.

"Yes, it was a startling discovery. But I was already aware that Chet Conroy had been in the business of selling stolen artifacts."

He rubbed his chin. "I recall now that I came back here one time and found some hunting books on the bookshelf, and my deck of cards lying out on the table. I assumed Chet had been here. He was the only other person who knew about this place."

"Speaking of card games, your ace of spades is missing," I said.

"Yeah, we just saw it at Conroy's Taxidermy shop," Forest added.

"I'm not surprised." Ray looked down. "And to add to the list of stolen goods, I suspect he's got my map. Without that, I have no clue where the pipe could be."

It was time to play *my* ace card. "I think we can help," I said. "Here's a sketch of the map that I made from your journal." I handed it to Ray.

"The building pictured is definitely the rangers'
lodge. Except whoever broke in may have already
found the artifact," I said.

"Not unless they were able to decipher the
code." He studied the map more closely. "This sentence—'Giin waa mikan zagaswe'idiwag opwaagan
dazhi makwa'—rings a bell. Certainly, too complicated
for the likes of Chet Conroy to solve; only someone
who speaks the native language would know what that
says."

He stared into space for a few minutes. Kneeling
by the bed, he reached under the mattress and pulled
out a small, worn pocketbook, placing it on the table.

"Something just clicked in my head. I recall now
that I used an Ojibwe dictionary for that line."

We watched anxiously as he flipped through the
pages.

"Let's start at the beginning." He handed me the
dictionary. "Dominic, please look up the word 'giin.'"

I quickly turned to the G page. "Giin means
'you.'"

"Okay. Now the second word, 'waa.'"

I flipped to the end of the book. U …V … W. "Waa means 'will.'" I was getting excited now.

"And the third word is 'mikan.'"

I backtracked to the M's. "Mikan means 'find.'"

Ray tipped back his head. "You will find …" He glanced at the map again. "This is a long one. 'Zagaswe'idiwag.'"

"Zag … what?" I took the map to see the word, then looked it up in the Z section. "That word means 'ceremonial.'"

Ray's eyes lit up. "We're almost there. What's next?"

"'Opwaagan.' It means … pipe!" I looked up the next word. "Dazhi means 'in.'"

"You will find the ceremonial pipe in …" I flipped to M for the last word, which was "makwa."

"Honey, I'm home!"

A gruff voice stopped our concentration. We looked up at the open hatch to see the barrel of Wade's rifle pointed in our direction. His face was flushed and he had a wild look in his eyes.

"Chet, is that you?" Ray stared up at Wade, shielding his eyes from the bright ray of sun that streamed down the shaft.

"You're living in the dark ages, pal. Chet was my dad. I'm Walter." His gaze landed on the book.

Walter? Who the heck is Walter?

"Here's what you're gonna do — you're gonna get up here and bring that book with ya."

Ray took the book out of my hands and tucked it into his back pocket, slowly making his way up the narrow steps. When he neared the top, he looked back at us and said, "Remember my name."

"No one's gonna remember you, old man." Wade grabbed Ray by the collar and jerked him out, pushing him aside.

He peered back down at us. "If ya don't wanna become bear-bait, ya better stay put. Adios, amigos." He winked at us before slamming the hatch shut.

CHAPTER 10

"This can't be happening." I ran up the stubby steps and pushed with all my might on the hatch. It wouldn't budge.

Forest and Sailor rushed to help. But even the three of us, precariously balanced on the steps, couldn't open it.

Sailor began banging on the hatch. "Help, help! We're trapped in here!"

Forest and I didn't add to the noise. It was useless. We made our way back down, dejectedly.

"Who was that guy, and what is he going to do with poor old Ray?" Sailor's voice quivered.

"Either Wade is a psychopath, or he has a twin brother," Forest deduced.

"He said his name was Walter, and that Chet was his dad." I sat at the table and buried my face in my hands. "Of course!" I looked up. "It's the guy I saw at

Gill's the other day. Wade said there was 'another side to the family business.' He must've been referring to Walter."

"Don't worry, Dominic." Sailor put her arm around my shoulder. "We'll find a way out."

"How do you figure?" Forest barked at her. "We're in a hole in the ground, and no one even knows we're here."

"Hmmm. What about Dominic's phone or the walkie-talkies?" She was ever the optimist.

"We can try, but I doubt we'll get a signal in this coffin."

Forest fished the walkie-talkie from his back pocket.

"We're trapped in a bunker!" he yelled into it. "Can anyone hear us? Hello?"

Dead silence.

I shook my head, unable to get through with my phone either.

"Are we going to die in here?" Sailor was visibly shaken; tears welled up in her eyes.

"No, that's not going to happen. Think about it. People built bunkers to live in for long periods of time," I said.

"That's right!" Forest exclaimed. "There must be some kind of ventilation. We just have to find it."

We ran to each corner of the bunker, searching high and low, but there was no vent in sight.

"Forest, help me move this bookshelf." I started tugging at one corner of the wooden box.

Forest began pulling on the opposite side. We dragged the shelf into the middle of the room.

"Well, well, what do we have here?" Forest pointed to a metal shaft in the ceiling above where the shelf had been.

I grabbed a chair and my flashlight and stood underneath the narrow vent. "Here goes nothing."

"What do you see?" Forest asked.

"It's pretty dark, even with the flashlight." I got down off the chair. "There's only one way out of here. One of us has to crawl through the vent."

Forest and I both looked at skinny little Sailor. It

looked like she was our only hope.

"How about you do it?" I asked her.

"I can't."

"Why not?"

"Because I don't want to."

We continued to stare her down.

"You expect *me* to crawl through *that*?" She slowly backed up. "What about Ray? He'll come back and help us."

"Sorry to burst your bubble, Sailor, but Ray might not be alive much longer, by the looks of Wade's rifle," Forest said.

"You mean Walter," I reminded him.

"Alright, then what does *Walter* want to do with a peace pipe?" Forest asked.

"Maybe sell it at the pawn shop?" I shrugged. "All I know is, we have to get out of here and find it before he does."

"Yeah, well don't forget, Walter has Ray *and* the codebook. I can't believe we were one word away from learning where Ray's secret hiding place was."

"Oh, yeah ..." I sat down on the chair.

"Didn't it seem like Ray was trying to tell us something? When he said, 'Remember my name,' it sounded like he was giving us a clue."

"Weird." Sailor began twirling her pigtails. "I wonder what that means. His name is Ray. How does that help us?"

We sat quietly for a few minutes.

"I've got it!" I jumped up from the chair. "Ray had a nickname when he was a kid. He said so in his journal."

"Running Bear!" Forest yelled.

I tapped my finger on my chin. "Okay. So ... bear, right? What's a bear got to do with this?"

"You-will-find-the-ceremonial-pipe-in-the... bear?" Sailor repeated the code translation.

"What the heck does that mean?" Forest asked. "How could a bear be running around with a pipe inside of him?"

I remembered my dream about the bear chasing me and the trunk in the woods. I realized the bear was very important, for some reason. I leaned over and picked up the map from the table where Ray had left it.

"We know Ray hid the pipe in the rangers' lodge." I pulled out my phone, studying the images again. One in particular stood out. "Look at this picture. Don't you find it odd that the paint is faded on this wall, and the carpet was all matted down? Looks like there used to be a large object standing there."

"Like a bear?" Sailor's eyebrows rose.

"You're a genius!" I shook her by the shoulders. "It has to be inside a taxidermy bear."

"Okay, but the bear is obviously gone. Where is it?" Forest asked.

We got quiet again.

"I'm pretty sure I saw one in the nature center!" I shouted. "They must've moved it."

"What do you want to bet, that's where Walter and Ray are headed? We need to get out of here!" Forest turned to Sailor. "Sis, you're going to have to crawl up that pipe. There's no other way."

"No, Forest! It's probably filthy. Besides, how do

you even know if I'll fit in there?"

"There's only one way to find out." He led her by the arm over to the vent. "At least try, okay?"

She sighed. "Okay. I'll do it."

"Forest, help me carry this table over to the vent, and then we'll put the chair on top." I cleared the cards and lifted one side. Together, we made it high enough for Sailor to reach the ceiling.

She climbed up on the chair and stuck her head inside. "It's dark in here!" Her voice echoed through the vent.

I grabbed the flashlight and shined it up inside.

"Yuck! There are spiders all over the place!" She gagged.

"Here, you can wear my baseball cap." I pulled it out of my backpack and handed it to her.

"Did you hear me? There are SPIDERS in there!" She held her hands over her eyes.

"I know. But you want to get out of here, don't you?" I asked.

"Yeah, and what about Ray? He needs our help."

Good old Forest. He knew his sister had a soft spot for the elderly. He used that to his advantage.

"Fine. Let's do this."

We helped Sailor up on the table, and then onto the chair. She began making her way into the vent.

"Yuck. Double yuck … gross!" She complained, but she continued the climb.

Forest and I worked together to lift her higher into the vent.

"Ewwww! There's a spider on my arm!"

"It won't hurt you, Sailor. Please keep going."

"Hey," she called down, "there's a wire thingie over the top."

"It's probably a vent cover. Try and push it out," Forest called up. "Push as hard as you can."

"I am," she whined. "It won't budge." She shrieked again; must have encountered another spider.

"Hold on. Let me see if I can find a screwdriver." I left Forest to hold the flashlight while I searched every nook and cranny in the bunker for a tool.

There was a small drawer next to a rusted basin.

I had to yank it pretty hard, but finally it flew open. No tools, but I managed to find a butter knife. I ran with it to the vent. "Here, take this. The mesh must be held together by screws. See if you can twist them open."

She reached down and grabbed the knife.

"Ew, ew, ew. Get off me, nasty bug!"

A few seconds later a screw came rattling down the vent walls, landing on the floor.

"You did it, Sailor! Keep going. You're almost there." Forest flashed a hopeful grin.

Another screw fell, and another. Finally, we could hear Sailor's gleeful cheer as she climbed out of the vent.

"Oh, no. Not good," she hollered down to us.

"What's wrong?" we shouted.

Her voice sounded muffled, and then we heard a scraping sound by the hatch. She ran back to the vent. "There's an axe stuck in the hatch handle. I can't get it out."

"Keep trying, Sailor!" Forest yelled up to her.

More scraping sounds came near the hatch door.

Then came a thud. Finally, the door opened.

We were greeted by Sailor's dirt-smudged, smiling face. I was never so relieved to see her.

"Umm, you might want to put that axe down, Sailor. You're scaring me," I said.

She took the axe and triumphantly swung it into a stump.

"Come on guys, let's go." I ran up ahead only to come face to face with the barrel of a gun.

CHAPTER 11

"What are *you* doing here?"

Still paralyzed by fear, I opened my eyes to see Ranger Rick lower his gun.

"You almost got yourself shot with a tranquilizer!" he scowled.

"Ranger, Walter just kidnapped Ray!" I shouted.

"Who the heck is Walter and Ray?" He lowered the gun.

Sailor ran up to him. "Walter is Wade Conroy's twin brother. He took Ray and the code book!"

"Huh?" Ranger Rick scratched his head. "What are they putting in the Kool-Aid these days?"

KWITCHHH …

"Ranger Rick, do you copy?" Static sounded from the radio that was clipped to his belt. He pressed the receiver.

"Go ahead."

"You got a bear in your back pocket."

KWITCHHH …

We stepped to the side, to see if anything was there. Behind the ranger emerged a gigantic black bear, walking on all fours.

"Sally, you're breaking up. Can you repeat … over." He adjusted the handle reception.

The sound of the radios agitated the bear. It looked at us, then rose onto hind legs, sniffing the air.

"Nobody move!" I nervously strained my voice.

Ranger Rick spun around on his heels in time to see the huge beast land back on the ground with a thud. It shook its burly neck back and forth with a huff.

"Ranger Rick!" I yelled. "Use your tranquilizer gun!"

"Way ahead of you, kid." He tilted the gun's muzzle toward the ground. "Just need to make sure it's loaded …"

The gun let off a loud "pop."

With a yelp, the ranger dropped the gun, grabbing his right foot. A tranquilizer dart was lodged through his shoe. Two seconds later, he tipped over, face-first into the dirt.

Fortunately, the sound of the gun going off scared the bear. It lumbered through the trees in the opposite direction.

We ran over to Ranger Rick, pushing him over onto his side. It looked as though he'd be okay, just passed out cold.

"He shot himself with his own gun—who does that?" Forest shook his head.

"That was a close one," I gasped.

"Yeah, but we're not out of the woods yet."

"Geez, Forest. Do you really have to make a joke at a time like this?" Sailor's knees were still knocking together.

"We need to get him out of here, somehow." I took Ranger Rick's radio in my hand, hoping I could reach Sally.

"Ranger Sally, this is Dominic. We need your assistance. Ranger Rick is hurt. Do you copy? Over …"

"10-4, Dominic. I'm already on my way." She

emerged from a clearing, took one look at the ranger, and rushed to his side.

"Come on, kids. Help me get him to the truck."

By now, Ranger Rick was starting to come to. We hoisted him to his feet, half-dragging him over to the DNR vehicle.

Once seated inside, Sally carefully tucked him in a blanket and closed the door. "I'm going to run the ranger over to the hospital. Hop in and I'll drop you three off at the campground first. We need to get you to safety."

"Gee, thanks," I said.

We threw our bikes in the cab and squeezed into the seat behind them.

"Time to put the hammer down." She squealed the tires onto the main highway.

"I know you have to take care of Ranger Rick, but how soon will you be back?" I asked.

"I'm not sure, sweet pea. Someone else is going to have to hold down the fort for a while."

Forest looked at me, eyebrows raised. I knew

what he was thinking. With Sally and Ranger Rick out of the picture, it was up to us to rescue Ray.

"I'm curious. Did there used to be a stuffed bear in the lodge?" I asked.

She made a right turn into the main entrance.

"I took it to the nature center last week. We needed to make room for some office furniture. Why do you ask?"

"No reason," I replied.

She pulled into the office parking lot. This would not do.

"Please, can you take us to the nature center? Please? It's an emergency!"

"Another emergency? You know, they do have a bathroom here in the office."

"No, it's not that. I'm dying of thirst!"

"Maybe you should cut down on your liquids. This is getting to be a real problem."

Ranger Rick tried to move his head. "A-a-um-a-a..." He tilted his head back and began snoring.

Sally squinted at him. "What's that? Sorry, but I

can't make out a word you're saying."

He was fast asleep.

"Okay, but why do I get the feeling you three are up to something?" She narrowed her eyes at us as she pulled back out onto the road.

In two minutes, we were there.

"Thanks for the lift," I called out behind me.

The parking lot was empty. The bear scare must've cleared the place out.

We edged along the building, creeping up to the nearest window to peer inside. At first glance, everything seemed to be in order. The taxidermy animals in the display were in place, and the magazines and brochures were neatly stacked on the counter.

"I feel like we're in a stakeout," Sailor blurted.

Forest groaned. "This *is* a stakeout, so be quiet."

We saw Walter rummaging through one of the displays. That was a good sign. It meant he hadn't found the peace pipe yet.

What wasn't a good sign, however, was Ray. He was tied up in ropes in the back corner, and from the looks of him, he'd been through the ringer. His tangled hair had been loosed from the ponytail. It looked like he had a black eye, too.

Walter's gun was propped up against the wall.

CHAPTER 12

"Doggone it, Ray. Where did you hide it?" Walter grumbled. He began to examine a stuffed raccoon, tipping it back and forth, his hand running all around it.

Ray moaned, glancing in Walter's direction. "I told you, Chet. I don't remember where I put it."

"Useless old codger. I'll just cut the whole thing up. What do I care?" He pulled a knife out from his back pocket and began cutting open the raccoon.

We ducked back down. "So, now what?" I whispered to Forest and Sailor.

"We go in and take Walter down!" Sailor held up two fists.

"Are you nuts!" Forest shook his head. "That guy has a rifle, and I'm pretty sure he's not afraid to use it."

"Maybe we could create a diversion to get Walter out of there so we can rescue Ray," I suggested.

Forest inched back up to the window. "Hey,

guys. Check it out—I think Ray's up to something!"

Sailor and I huddled in next to Forest.

Sure enough, Ray's hands were rigorously moving behind his back. "Looks like he's trying to untie himself," I whispered. "This should be good."

I silently cheered for Ray, but as frail as he looked, there didn't seem to be much hope.

Suddenly, his left hand became free. He quickly untangled his right hand, and then worked on loosening his feet. He nervously kept his eyes on Walter, freezing perfectly still whenever Walter so much as flinched in his direction.

"I bet you thought you were clever, using my dad's taxidermy book to figure out how to hide the pipe in one of his hunting trophies," Walter said.

He had moved on to another display and was inspecting the back end of a stuffed mink, shaking it up and down.

Ray inched himself backwards toward the pile of cookware Ranger Rick left behind after the safety demonstration. We saw him grab a heavy cast iron skillet, hiding it behind his back.

When he spotted us in the window, Ray smiled and nodded. We gave him a thumbs-up. All we could do was wait. My heart felt like it was going to jump right out of my chest.

Walter was so preoccupied with trying to find the peace pipe that he had no clue what Ray was up to.

"This has gotta be the big bonanza!" Walter finally caught sight of the taxidermy bear mount on the other side of the nature center. He bent low to look over the stitching on the bear's underbelly.

This was Ray's chance. He quickly crept up behind Walter with the frying pan.

Walter turned just in time to see Ray raising the pan high in the air. He walloped Walter over the head, knocking him out cold.

I sprang to my feet. "Let's go, guys."

We ran to the side door and went in.

"Ray!" Sailor ran up to him and gave him a tight hug. "We're here to rescue you!"

"Thank you, little miss, but I don't think he'll be

much trouble now." Ray observed a motionless Walter.

"Stop right there," a man's voice boomed from the back of the room. It was Wade. He took one look at Walter lying on the floor and rushed to his side.

"What have you done?" he bellowed at Ray. He picked up the rifle that was leaning against the wall.

Ray nervously dropped the skillet, which sounded with a loud clatter on the floor.

Oh, dear Lord. What now?

Ray quickly regained his composure. "I'll tell you what I've done, I gave him what he deserves—that's what!" He shook his finger at Wade.

"You're obviously a Conroy; Walter's twin, no less. Surely you heard what your dad, Chet, did to me at this park. He bushwhacked me, hit me over the head with my axe. I suffered from amnesia all these years, and for what? All because I caught him stealing Chief Mexico's peace pipe."

"That's what your brother was searching for inside that bear just now," I confirmed.

Wade stood over Walter, who was starting to

moan and rub the back of his head. "Walter, you prodigal nincompoop! What have you gone and done?"

Walter turned on his side, his eyes starting to flutter. "Come on, Bro. That no-good lumberjack stole the peace pipe from us! Dad had it first. He traded those robbers for it all those years ago. I just want what's rightfully ours."

Wade looked to Ray. "Is that true?"

"Yes, it's the truth. But that doesn't make it right. That pipe doesn't belong to any of you. It belongs to Chief Mexico's tribe, the Potawatomi." Ray clumsily tied his hair back into a ponytail. "Your family is just out to make a lousy buck."

Wade turned to Walter. "How did you even get involved in this?"

Walter looked at the floor. "I saw the old man's write-up in the newspaper, and then I remembered that Pop showed us that bunker when we were kids. Figured I might find a clue inside as to where the pipe was."

"I'm embarrassed to be your brother. What are

you, some kind of degenerate redneck? Get off the floor, Walt." Wade tapped him with his foot. "Come on, I said get up!"

Walter slowly stood to his feet, all the while holding his head. "Pop was the one who had his heart set on that pipe to add to his collection. All I ever wanted was to carry on his legacy, but you wouldn't understand. You were too busy playing with your dress-up dolls."

"At least what I do is respectable."

Their sibling rivalry was almost as bad as Forest and Sailor's.

"Mr. Conroy?" I approached Wade. "How did you know your brother kidnapped Ray and brought him here, in the first place?"

Walter glared at us. "*You* kids—haven't you meddled enough in other people's business?"

Ray stomped his foot. "Listen here, mister. If it weren't for these kids, we wouldn't be any closer to finding the peace pipe than your dad was."

"Honestly, I didn't know anything about it,"

Wade said. "Walter told me he was coming here to hunt a bear, and I thought he might need my help. In fact, I have the bear caged right now in the back of my pickup. I was looking for Ranger Rick so he could transfer it further north, and this is what I found instead."

"Ooh, well Ranger Rick shot himself in the foot with a tranquilizer gun and Sally took him to the hospital," Forest explained.

"That sounds about right," Wade chuckled.

"Sir? What about the peace pipe? Can we look for it?" Forest asked Ray.

"The tribes have protocol, and because of how old it is, I don't think it would be wise for us to try and handle it." He picked up the mounted bear and was about to set it against the wall, when a portion of leathery pelt fell down from its side.

We all stared inside the large incision, and there it was! The pipe had a long, wooden stem, hollow and smooth. It was decorated with feathers and porcupine quills, with a carved stone bowl on one end, set on top.

"Tell you what." Ray looked at the three of us. "After I contact the Potawatomi tribe, I'm going to let them know that you kids played an important role in finding Chief Mexico's peace pipe and restoring a part of their history."

Wade pulled on his beard. "And what do you suppose I do with my renegade brother?"

"I'm willing to 'bury the hatchet' so to speak, if he's willing to surrender the rest of his collection." Ray eyed up Walter.

"Anything is better than doing time in the clink." Walter seemed willing.

"And I'll see to it that he does," Wade agreed.

"How are we going to explain all of this to GB and Windsong?" I turned to Forest and Sailor. "Our grandparents are going to hit the roof when they find out."

"I'm an expert on peacekeeping. I learned from the best of them," Ray said. "Leave that to me."

CHAPTER 13

GB pulled into the Aurora Medical Center parking lot on the outskirts of the town of Two Rivers. It was an impressive red-brick building with teal-tinted windows and trim.

"I don't see why we have to visit Ranger Rick," Forest complained. "It's not our fault he shot himself in the foot."

"Aha, well think of it as your penance for not telling us what the three of you were up to all this while." GB looked back at us from the rearview mirror.

"And it's the right thing to do," Windsong added. "He was trying to keep everyone safe, after all." She looped her beaded purse over her shoulder and stepped out of the truck.

Forest, Sailor and I exited from the back and waited for GB to lock up. After stopping at the receptionist desk to find out which room Ranger Rick was in, we headed up a long flight of stairs. GB was pretty winded when we finally got to the top. He mopped his forehead with his handkerchief.

"You know, you could've taken the elevator," I pointed out to GB. "It was right next to the stairs."

"Gee, thanks, Dominic," he muttered.

We made our way down the hall.

"Here it is, 331." Sailor peeked her head into the room. "Hi Ranger!"

Forest and I followed her in. Ranger Rick was lying in the bed, looking pale, his hair an unruly mess. Ranger Sally was holding a cup with a straw up to him. He pushed the cup aside.

"What are *you* kids doing here?" He sat up in his bed with a scowl on his face. "Can't a guy get some peace?"

"Well, hello, Ranger." Windsong and GB walked in behind us.

The ranger's face colored. "Ah … hello. I wasn't expecting visitors." He grabbed his Stetson hat from the bedside table and stuffed it on his head, which looked silly with the hospital gown he was wearing.

"I hope it's okay that we stopped in. We were worried about you." Windsong walked over to him and patted his hand.

"Heavens, yes, it's more than okay. It's good of you to check up on an injured friend," Sally gushed. From the looks of it, she had dipped her face in a bucket of paint. The last time I saw that much lipstick and eyeshadow was in a girlie magazine.

"That's why we bought chocolates," Forest said.

Ranger Rick eyed him over. "Well, where are they?"

"Oh, we ate them as our reward for visiting you."

"Forest Everly, what an awful thing to say!" Windsong tapped him on the head. Forest jerked away, brushing his long bangs out of his eyes.

The ranger glanced in our direction. "I hear there was some foul play going on at the park just like you kids said. That campground will turn into a circus if I'm not there to keep an eye on things."

"Yeah," Forest whispered in my ear, "he's really gonna put his foot down when he gets back."

I didn't dare make a sound or even crack a smile. Forest was in enough trouble already.

"So, Ranger, when will you be back to Point Beach?" GB quickly changed the subject.

"Not soon enough," he sputtered.

"Indeed." GB stroked his mustache.

A petite nurse in pink scrubs walked in with a small paper cup in hand. "Time for your pills, Mr. Rick."

GB ushered us to the door. "Well, kids, what do you say we head over to the Spirit of the Rivers memorial? There's just enough time before we head home. I have a little surprise for you."

"What is it, what is it?" Sailor jumped up and down.

"Patience, my dear. You'll see very soon." Windsong winked at her.

I led the way to the elevator. Figured I'd save GB the trouble of working up another sweat.

The sun beat down on Lake Michigan, casting shadows of clouds over the sparkling, blue water. A few seagulls circled overhead. We drove up to the parking lot on the other side of the boulevard and walked along the Mariner's Trail.

On the shoreline, a massive bronze sculpture loomed before us. The inscription read "Spirit of the Rivers: A tribute to the Woodland Natives of the Upper Great Lakes."

The memorial consisted of three 10-foot figures: A man carrying a birch bark canoe, his strong arms and torso lifting the vessel high overhead. On one side of him, there was a woman with their belongings strapped to her back. On the opposite side, the statue of an elder, showing them the way.

"Impressive, don't you think?"

We turned to see Ray, standing alongside the monument. He was leaning on his cane but looked well-rested, despite yesterday's ordeal; the black bruise under his eye fading to purple.

"It was built by Manitowoc native, R.T. Wallen, to honor the people who lived here before us. In fact, the name 'Manitowoc' means 'Home of the Great Spirit' in their language."

He tipped his cane toward a woman sitting on a bench nearby. "I'd like you to meet Chenoa from the Potawatomi Tribe in Crandon."

The woman stood and approached us. "Hello, everyone." She smiled, extending her hand in welcome. "Thank you for recovering my ancestor's peace pipe."

Her stoic features and soulful brown eyes were mesmerizing. It was a sense of accomplishment, knowing that the artifact, finally, after all these years, resided with its rightful owners.

"That's not all they recovered. These kids helped me remember my roots," Ray stated. "Chenoa wants to reconnect me to my great-grandmother Wawetseka's relatives, and I may even write poetry again."

"Well, I reckon they were happy to help," GB admitted. "My grandson seems to have a knack for solving mysteries at Point Beach."

"So true." Windsong beamed with pride at Forest and Sailor. "How great it is, that this next generation had an opportunity to learn about the past and try to make things better."

"We look back so that we can see ahead," Chenoa agreed. "It's important to examine our lives and make sure we are being respectful of all living things."

Ray stared into the distance at a handful of workers who were pulling weeds and cutting down old growth; others were digging with shovels.

"Reminds me of being a lumberjack — it was hard work, but for as many trees as we cut down, we always planted a new seedling. It gave nature a chance to start over again, just like the volunteers cleaning up Forget-Me-Not Creek."

He nodded in their direction. "This basically unknown little stream was blocked by rocks and invasive shrubs while the developing area was being excavated, but now it will be restored again."

"Very good, Running Bear." Chenoa nodded. "Just as smoke rises from the ceremonial pipe offering up prayers for peace, we have been taught that every step taken upon the earth should be as a prayer."

"Wonderful to meet you, Chenoa. It's like a dream come true." Windsong graciously added to our farewells.

As we parted ways, I glanced down the path that weaved around the mouth of the creek where it spilled into the lake. Something caught my attention.

"Hey, look at those little blue flowers—" I bent down to inspect a tuft of foliage along the shore of the trickling stream. "Just like in my dream—it *is* like a dream come true!"

"That's right, Dominic." Windsong put her arm around me. "Everything in your dream came to pass— the bear, the metal trunk, which turned out to be the bunker, the rusted arrow which symbolized the Native Americans who were here before us, and even the forget-me-nots, which are right where this journey ends."

"Well, I'll be." GB tilted his head toward the tiny blue flowers. "Forget-me-nots."

We walked the Mariner's Trail to take in a few more rays of sun and beauty. Above us circled a bald eagle. We watched the magnificent bird soar across the sky.

It was the perfect ending to solving another mystery at Point Beach.

Debby lives in Maribel, Wisconsin. She's a member of Pens of Praise Christian writers' group and enjoys family gatherings, country life and the four seasons.

Kate lives in Branch, Wisconsin. She's a member of Pens of Praise Christian writers' group and a church accompanist. She enjoys spending time with her family.

Connect with us online at:

Facebook.com/MysteryatPointBeach

Facebook.com/TheTinCanSeries

Our thanks to Anne Bender for all the encouragement and insight, Ben Wolf for his genius ideas, Laura Skup Gomez (Windsong) for joining us on the journey, Sarah Grosskopf for editing, and Nathaniel Gerhardt, museum cultural educator at the Oneida Nation Museum, for the history lesson.

Books in the Mystery at Point Beach Series:

Book 1: Sundae Wars

Book 2: Pirate's Booty

Book 3: Alien Invasion

Book 4: Bushwhacked

Book 5: The Ringmaster

Book 6: Haunted Hemlock

Books in The Tin Can Series:

Book 1: Mystery at Flamingo Bay